On the Road

Adapted by Kitty Richards

Based on the series created by Michael Poryes and Rich Correll & Barry O'Brien

Part One is based on the episode, "Get Down Study-udy-udy," Written by Andrew Green

Part Two is based on the episode, "I Want You To Want Me . . . To Go To Florida," Written by Michael Poryes

DISNEP PRESS

New York

PART ONE

Chapter One

Another amazing Hannah Montana concert was coming to an end. Miley Stewart, wearing her long, blond Hannah wig, danced along with two of her backup dancers as she belted out the last lines of her hit song "Nobody's Perfect."

When Miley was through, she stood in front of the audience as they cheered and cheered. Looking out into the crowd, she spotted a WE ♥ U HANNAH sign. She grinned. Her fans were too much! She knew that she was, without question, the luckiest pop star on the planet—with the greatest fans ever.

"Thank you! You guys rock!" Miley cried. "Keep on listening, and I'll see you guys when I get back from my very first European tour!" The crowd roared. "I know! I can't wait!" She began to list all her favorite European things: "Swiss chocolate, Italian shoes, and French boys!" She smiled. "Ooh, la la!"

Miley's dad, Mr. Stewart, stood in the wings wearing his manager's disguise, complete with itchy, fake mustache. He frowned. French boys? He didn't think so! "Ooh, la la, uh-uh-uh," he told a stagehand as he crossed off part of Hannah's itinerary. "The closest she's coming to Paris is Paris, Texas!"

* * *

The next morning Jackson Stewart, Miley's brother, was hard at work taking care of some personal hygiene before school. That's right, it was toenail-clipping day. Jackson sat on the sofa wearing goggles, his bare foot propped up on the coffee table next to a small gong. "Nailed it!" he said proudly as he neatly clipped off a nail. He held the clipper up to his mouth like a microphone. "Now-ow-ow," he pronounced, echoing his voice in order to sound like a ringside announcer at a boxing match, "for the main event-ent-ent-ent! The big toe-oe-oe." He bent over his foot and got to work.

Gong! As luck would have it, his dad walked through the front door just as the clipped nail ricocheted off the gong. Most unfortunately for Mr. Stewart, it landed right in his eye. "Ow!" he cried. He held the day's mail in one hand and rubbed his eye with the other. "Dang it, Jackson!" he said. "I hate toenail day!"

Jackson looked up from his work. "Hey, I put a note on the refrigerator. If you choose not to wear your protective goggles, I can't be held responsible." He shook his head at such foolishness.

Mr. Stewart pointed to the mail. "Well here's something you *can* be held responsible for," he said. "Looks like this letter is from your school." He began to rip open the envelope.

"Oh, man," said Jackson, his heart sinking. This couldn't be good.

Mr. Stewart's brow furrowed as he began to read the letter. "Oh, boy," he said.

Jackson gave his dad a sugary sweet smile. In his experience, letters from school never brought good news. It was time to start with some serious flattery. "Did I tell you how great your hair looks?" he asked. "It's like a field of wheat. How do you keep it so lush?"

Mr. Stewart shook his head. Jackson was off the hook. "It's about Miley," he explained. "And I use a volumizing mousse. But just a dab, right here in the palm, then you—" He rubbed his hands together to show his son his exact technique.

"Sorry, Dad," Jackson said dismissively, raising his hands. "I only care if I'm in trouble."

Just then Miley came down the stairs into the living room, doing a conga-line dance as she sang her "I'm Going to Europe" song.

"London, England; Paris, France;
Watch me do my Europe dance!
Europe, Europe, Europe!
I'm going to Europe!"

Miley ended her little performance by bumping hips with her dad. Gone was the flashy costume and long, blond wig from last night. She was back to her everyday look. Her brown hair was loose and wavy, and she wore long, dark denim shorts with cuffs and a hooded red sweater over a white shirt.

"Yeah, about that," Mr. Stewart said. "I just got this letter from school and . . ."

A letter from school could only mean one thing—Jackson was in trouble again. Miley turned to her brother and did the "shame, shame" thing with her fingers as she finished her dad's sentence. ". . . somebody's grades are slipping again? Jackson, Jackson, Jackson. What are we going to do with you, boy?"

Miley was digging a hole for herself a mile wide! Jackson tried to warn his sister. "Uh, Mile—"

But he was interrupted by his dad. "No son," Mr. Stewart said with a smile. "Let her go on." He was enjoying this! He handed her the letter. "How would you handle this, Miley?"

Miley shook her head sadly. "Well, Dad, as much as it pains me, I'd have to say: no grades, no Europe." She reached over and patted Jackson on the chest. "I'll miss you buddy."

Then she glanced down at the letter. Her eyes flew open as she realized that the Stewart who was in trouble this time was *her*. Yikes! It was time to backpedal—and fast! "Then again, what do I know? I'm just a kid!" She turned to her dad, a big fake smile plastered across her face. "Have I told you your hair looks great today?"

Jackson shook his head. "I already tried field of wheat—good luck."

"So lush," said Miley, reaching up to touch it. But she had a sinking feeling that flattery wasn't going to work. Not this time.

Chapter Two

Later that day, Miley and her two best friends, Lilly Truscott and Oliver Oken, had just finished their lunch and were tossing their empty lunch bags into the trash.

"How can your dad cancel your European tour just because of one bad grade?" Oliver asked Miley quietly, so the other students wouldn't overhear. Oliver and Lilly were the only two who knew about Miley's double life as a pop star. She liked her life at school just the way it was—normal. Or as normal as the life of a girl with a secret pop-star identity could be.

Lilly piped up. "Umm, I guess it went something like, 'Bud, you're not goin',' " she said in her best Southern accent. "And then he probably said something about your Uncle Earl's feet."

Miley shook her head. "It's so weird," she said. "It's like you were there."

As they walked through the quad, Miley glanced around. "Look at this," she said, pointing at the food that various students were eating. "*English* muffins. *Italian* sausages. *Swiss* cheese." Her voice began to rise. "Why are all of you taunting me?" Suddenly she realized everyone was staring at her. "Sorry. Little cranky. Skipped breakfast," she explained. "Most important meal of the day. Carry on."

Lilly was very unhappy. "Man, your dad is being so unfair!" she cried. Then she pulled out a red beret and placed it on her head at a jaunty angle. "I already bought this beret. See, so cute!"

Miley sighed. The beret *was* cute. But her dad meant business. There was no way around it. She knew how upset her friends were that the trip was in jeopardy. The two often traveled with Miley, assuming fake identities as well so no one would figure out her secret—Lilly as Lola Luftnagle and Oliver as Mike Standley III. If she couldn't pull up her grades—and fast—Lola and Mike were in for some major disappointment.

The end-of-lunch bell rang, and the three friends paused for a moment near a bank of lockers before heading to their respective classes.

"Listen guys," began Miley. "It's not my

dad's fault. We have a deal. School always comes first. And if I can't pull at least a B in biology, the closest thing we'll get to Paris is ordering . . ." She paused to put on a *tres* fake French accent. "French toast," she finished.

Lilly's eyes widened. No taking pictures from the top of the Eiffel Tower? No shopping on the Champs-Élysées? No strolling on the banks of the Seine River? This was too awful for words!

"Hold up," said Oliver, thinking fast. "If you need a B, all you have to do is ace the midterm tomorrow." It was so simple! He turned to Lilly. "How did she miss that? No wonder she's flunking biology!" he whispered.

Miley rolled her eyes. She had had enough. She grabbed Oliver by the front of his shirt and yanked him toward her.

"Ow!" he cried.

"If I could ace the midterm," Miley explained through gritted teeth, "I wouldn't have a problem, would I?" She let him go.

"And if I stay friends with you, I'll never have chest hair, will I?" Oliver asked, rubbing his chest.

Spanish class was over. Jackson walked down the stairs with Becky, a cute blond girl from his class. She was having trouble in Spanish, and Jackson knew just how to fix it.

"So you just come over to my house after school," he said. "I'll be happy to help you with your Spanish. *Mi casa*," he said, pointing to himself, "*es su casa*," he finished, pointing to her.

"What does that mean?" Becky wanted to know.

Jackson grimaced. "It means we have a lot of work to do," he explained.

"Thanks so much, Jackson. I really appreciate it," Becky said. "I really, really appreciate it," she added flirtatiously.

"*No problemo*," said Jackson with a smile.

Becky wrinkled her brow in thought. "*Problemo*. Wait, I know this one. . . ."

"Okay," Jackson replied quickly. "We'll just go over it later."

"I can't wait!" Becky said with a smile as she headed down the hallway.

"*Ay, caramba*," Jackson said, shaking his head. He certainly had his work cut out for him! He walked over to the quad and sat down next to a big kid with curly, blond hair wearing a football jersey. It was Thor, Jackson's new friend, who had recently moved to California from Mooville, Minnesota. Thor had a thick midwestern accent and had grown up on a farm, where his only friends were cows. Even though Thor never failed to embarrass him, Jackson still had a soft spot for the kid, mostly because Jackson remembered in vivid detail just what it was like to be the new kid in school, friendless and not fitting in. He and his family had relocated from Tennessee not all that long ago for Miley's career, so he often offered Thor advice on how to be more "California."

"Hey, Thor, whassup?" Jackson asked.

Thor turned to Jackson with big, sad eyes. "Oh, Jackson, it's Old Snowball," he said dejectedly. "The landlord says we have to get rid of him, and how can I do that? I love him *soooo* much. I mean Old Snowball, not the landlord, although he seems very nice," he continued, all in a rush. He threw his arms around Jackson. "I need a hug!"

Yikes! Thor needed some California lessons, and quick! Jackson simultaneously jumped up and pushed Thor away. "Whoa Thor, in California, when a guy says 'whassup?' the other guy says 'not much' and we move on," he explained.

"Oh, Thor, you dumb bunny," said Thor, shaking his head. Was he ever going to learn? "Let's try it again."

"Good," said Jackson. He humored Thor by getting up and then immediately sitting back down again. "Hey, Thor, whassup?" he repeated.

Once again, Thor threw his arms around Jackson. "Oh, Jackson, the landlord says . . ."

Jackson pushed his friend away. "Whoa, whoa, whoa! We don't hug," he said, exasperatedly. "We occasionally slap butts — but only on the football field."

Thor thought for a moment. "Oh, then

I owe the janitor an apology," he said.

Jackson's voice softened. "Look, if you need a place to park the old guy, he can stay at my house," he said.

Thor's face lit up. "Snowball, did you hear that?" he cried. "We found you a home! Come on, boy!"

Jackson was confused. "You brought your dog to school?"

"Oh, Snowball's not a dog," explained Thor.

Just then a white parrot landed on Jackson's shoulder. "Moo!" it said. Jackson was speechless.

"Or a cow," said Thor. "Stop showing off," he scolded the parrot good-naturedly. "You're not fooling anyone."

Jackson stared at the white bird out of the corner of his eye. He had a feeling he was in for more than he had bargained for.

Lilly and Oliver had been waiting anxiously for Miley outside of the dreaded biology classroom. They grabbed her as soon as she appeared and pulled her to the side for an update.

"Okay, we've got a plan," Lilly told her.

"But if you don't like it, it was all her idea," said Oliver, pointing to Lilly. He then covered his chest protectively.

"Way to sell it, Oliver," said Lilly, rolling her eyes.

"Hey, I've only got one chest hair, and I need it for gym class," Oliver protested.

Lilly turned to Miley, "Just ask the smartest kid in the class to tutor you," she explained.

"Are you kidding me?" Miley spluttered. "The smartest kid in the class is . . ."

The three friends watched as Rico—aka the Lonely Little Munchkin, Little Devil,

Mini Me, Rinkadink, Shortstack, Teeny-weeny Meanie, and the Evil Little Boy, to name a few of his many nicknames — walked past them into the classroom. Rico was at least a head and a half shorter than the other students in the class, as he had skipped several grades. He was also, quite possibly, the most annoying kid in school, if not the planet. He was with their teacher, Ms. Kunkle, who had her nose buried in a report. Rico, wearing a black-and-white camo vest, seemed frustrated.

"How can you not get this?" Rico asked the teacher, putting his hand to his head.

"I'm sorry," replied Ms. Kunkle. "It's just that your data suggests ten percent of human genes vary in the number of copies of specific DNA segments."

Rico rolled his eyes. "Exactly! This isn't brain surgery!"

Miley looked at her friends in disbelief. "Are you serious? You want me to ask Rico?" It was almost too much to bear. "Come on, it's not like he's the only kid with a brain in this class." The three peeked into the classroom and took a look around. A girl with braids was balancing a pencil on her nose. Another girl was curling her eyelashes. A boy was playing with one of his sneakers. One girl made her fingers into goalposts as the boy at the desk behind her flicked a tiny, folded paper football to score a field goal. It wasn't even close. No geniuses of any kind in this bunch!

"Okay, fine," Miley said. Against her better judgment, she took a deep breath and marched over to Rico. Lilly was right on her heels. "Ohhh, Rico," Miley said, playing with her hair.

Rico looked up. "Hey Bubble Brain,"

he replied. "How's it going?"

Miley sat in an empty desk next to Rico. This wasn't going to be easy! "Aw, smart, funny . . ." she said with a fake laugh as she began to list his attributes.

"And dead-on about the bubble brain," Lilly finished.

Miley gave her a look. It wasn't a friendly one.

"But just in biology," Lilly quickly added. "Other than that, you're as sharp as a tick."

"That's 'tack,'" Miley corrected.

"Ya see?" said Lilly, clearly pleased at her friend's intelligence.

Rico shook his head. "Good thing you two are pretty," he said condescendingly.

Miley gritted her teeth. Paris, think of Paris, she told herself. "Okay, I'm just going to come right out and ask you—" she began.

Rico cut to the chase. "You need help in biology," he said with a nod.

Miley was caught off guard. "How'd you know that?" she asked.

Rico rolled his eyes. "Please. Put together the grades from your last four quizzes and they spell 'duh-duh-duh-ff.'"

"Hey, one of those was a duh-duh-duh plus," Miley argued weakly.

"Whatever," said Rico dismissively. "I'll help you." He paused for effect. "If you help me with another class."

Now this was more like it! Miley smiled at Lilly, proud as a peacock. "How about them apples?" she crowed. "The genius needs *my* help." She turned to Rico. "So what can I do for you?"

Rico just grinned.

Chapter Three

Miley looked ridiculous. She balanced a large globe in her hand and was clad in a long, fancy pink dress with a supertight bodice and an enormous hoopskirt. But most outlandish of all was the towering wig she wore on her head. It was at least three feet high and looked as if it were spun out of blond sugar. She couldn't remember the last time she felt so uncomfortable! She glanced over at Rico. He looked pretty silly himself, wearing a velvet hat with a feather, a flowing shirt, a vest, short pants, and tights. He brandished a paintbrush and a palette in his hands as he put the finishing touches on his painting.

But Miley wasn't holding the globe to Rico's liking. "Higher . . . higher . . ." he directed. "Lower. I'm sorry, lower . . . yeah, ah, that's good."

"That's where I started," complained Miley. "Come on, Rico. I've been standing like this for two hours. Ugh, my neck is cramping." She tilted her neck to stretch it. "And this wig is really heavy!" she cried as she lost her balance and toppled to the floor.

"Don't worry about it," said Rico. "My masterpiece is complete!"

Miley rolled herself over to a nearby desk. She grabbed on to it and unsteadily struggled to her feet.

"Finally," she said, adjusting her wig.

"Now . . ." She took a look at Rico's painting. "What's this?" she demanded.

Rico's canvas depicted just one thing — the globe.

"An A-plus," he said proudly.

"So what was I here for?" Miley wanted to know.

"I needed someone to hold the globe," explained Rico.

Miley couldn't believe her ears! This was low, even for Rico. "What about this stupid outfit?" she asked.

"That was just a little something for Rico," he said with a wink.

Miley was furious. "I'm gonna give Rico a little something if you don't teach me some biology!" she growled.

"Okay, okay, fine," said Rico with a sigh. "I will give you the secret to my success. But share this with no one."

Now she was getting somewhere! "Yeah, sure, whatever, teach me," said Miley. She and Rico sat down in front of Miley's biology textbook at the desk. Rico set his palette down next to it.

"Okay, open the book," instructed Rico.

Miley leaned forward, holding the towering wig with one hand so it wouldn't fall over. "Check," she said.

"Close the book," said Rico.

Miley was confused. "What?" she asked.

"That's it," said Rico, giving Miley a thumbs-up. "Good luck on the test." He picked up his palette and stood up to leave. Miley stared at Rico in disbelief, then grabbed him.

"But you didn't teach me anything," she protested.

"Don't you have a photographic memory like me?" asked Rico.

"No," replied Miley.

Rico shook his head. "Then you're on your own, toots." He left the art room, taking his palette and his floppy feathered hat with him.

"Wait a minute!" shouted Miley. Rico wasn't going to get away with this! "Get back here!" She stood up, intending to chase after him, but her large skirt prevented her from getting through the door. She thought for a moment, then smiled. Rico wasn't the only one with brains— she'd go through sideways! She backed up, tilted her head to lower her wig . . . and then lost her balance. "Not agaaaaain!" she yelped as she fell to the floor with a crash. So much for *that* idea!

Later in the day, Thor brought Snowball to Jackson's house. The two stood in the kitchen, Snowball's gilded cage sitting on the counter between them. Thor was having a hard time saying good-bye and was giving Jackson painfully detailed instructions on how to care for his beloved pet.

"At bedtime," explained Thor, "he loves it when you read *Goodnight Moon*." He lowered his voice. "And don't show him where the mouse is, just let him find it."

"Right. Got it," Jackson said dismissively. "Now if you don't mind, I've got a study date with Becky, so . . ." he steered Thor toward the door.

Thor stopped. "Oh, you mean Becky with the bad breath?" he asked.

"No, not her!" cried Jackson.

Thor thought for a moment. "Oh, you mean Bucktooth Becky, the human bottle-opener?" he asked. "She scares me. Although, she did come in handy on that field trip." He laughed at the memory.

"No," said Jackson. "Becky from Spanish class."

"Ohhhhhh," said Thor, nodding his head. "You mean Brainless Becky."

"Yes," said Jackson. "Brainless, Bodacious Becky." He leaned back and grinned, pleased with himself.

The doorbell rang. Jackson's study date had arrived.

"Ah," said Jackson. Then he called out, "*Uno momento, señorita!*"

"What?" cried Becky.

"I'll be right there!" Jackson shouted. He turned to Thor. "Use the back door," he told him.

"Okay," replied Thor. He turned to Snowball. Now this really was good-bye. "Bye-bye," he said sadly.

"Bye-bye," Snowball called back.

"Bye-bye," said Thor again, unable to leave or pull himself away from his parrot.

"Bye-bye," Snowball replied.

Jackson had had enough. "Just get outta here already!" he cried impatiently.

"Oh, and if he gets too cold, here's his little parka," Thor remembered, pulling a tiny pink jacket out of his back pocket. "Don't zip it up. He likes to do it himself," he explained, close to tears.

Thor finally left. Jackson stuck the jacket between the bars of the cage as he made his way to the front door. "Likes to zip it himself," Jackson muttered as he went. "Right."

Just then Jackson heard a tiny zipping sound. He spun around to find Snowball wearing his jacket, fully fastened. The hood was even up.

Jackson shook his head. What a weird little bird!

Jackson's tutoring session was going very well. He and Becky sat on the couch, huddled over the same Spanish textbook.

"*Louisa tiene catarro,*" said Becky.

"*Excelente!*" cried Jackson, proud of his student.

"You're such a good teacher," Becky gushed. "I just have one question." She smiled. "How do you say 'kiss me' in Spanish?"

"Oh, that's easy!" Jackson said automatically. "It's . . ." then he paused, realizing what Becky meant. "Ohhhh," he said happily. The two moved toward each other. Closer . . . closer . . . then just as their lips were about to touch, a small voice broke the silence. "Bucktooth Becky!" it said. It was Snowball!

"What?" said Becky, confused.

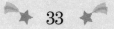

"Ah, just ignore him," said Jackson quickly, eager to return to the business at hand.

"Becky with the bad breath," Snowball continued.

Becky covered her mouth with her hands. "Why is he saying that?" she asked, upset.

"He's a bird," explained Jackson. "He just repeats what he hears." He scrambled to Snowball's side.

"Shut up," he whispered urgently to the bird.

"So where'd he hear it?" Becky's eyes narrowed.

"Brainless Becky, Brainless Becky," chanted Snowball.

Oh, no! Jackson wanted to strangle the parrot. Things were going from bad to worse!

"What?" exclaimed Becky.

"I did not say that," Jackson explained. "I said, 'Brainless, *Bodacious* Becky.'" Oops. *That* was the wrong thing to say. Jackson knew he was in trouble now.

"Excuse me?" said Becky. She stood up and faced Jackson, her face turning red.

"Bye-bye," said Snowball pleasantly.

Becky was furious. "Bye-bye is right," she said to Jackson. "You blew it, jerk."

"No wait!" cried Jackson. "You don't understand!" He thought fast. "Ah, bodacious is Spanish for smart, from the Latin root *braindacious*!"

But it was no use—she wasn't buying it. Turned out she was not as brainless as everyone seemed to think. It was *adios* for Becky. She didn't even close the door behind her.

Chapter Four

Later that night, Mr. Stewart strummed his guitar in the kitchen. He was not only Hannah Montana's manager and producer, but he also wrote most of Hannah's songs. Back in the day, he had been a country-music star—Robby Ray, the Honky Tonk Heartthrob. He was singing a modified version of one of his songs to Snowball:

"I want my mullet back."

Snowball took the next two lines:

"My messy cage and my eight track.

My swinging perch and my water bowl."

Mr. Stewart and Snowball sang the last line together.

"Now Rob and Snowy gonna rock'n'roll."

"Dad!" Miley called from the living room. "Can you keep it down in there? I'm trying to study!" She shook her head and returned to her biology textbook.

"I'm sorry, honey," said Mr. Stewart. "All right, Snowball, we're going to take five. When I get back I'm teaching you 'Wanna Be Your Joe.'"

"Robby rocks," squawked Snowball.

"And don't you forget it," replied Mr. Stewart with a wink. He smiled. "I love that bird."

Miley, meanwhile, was cramming like

crazy. But it just didn't seem to be working. She pointed to her ribs. "Ribs attach to . . ." she began, pointing to her chest. "Sacrum," she said. She frowned. That wasn't right. "No, sternum," she corrected herself. "Which attach to . . ." She pointed to her collarbone. Um, what was it called? "A bone that ends in 'illa' or 'uno.'" She thought and thought, but it wasn't coming to her. This was so frustrating! "Or Oprah!" she shouted, throwing her hands in the air in defeat. "Yeah that's it. It's my 'Oprah,' and I'm a 'dope-ra' who's never going to 'Europa'!" She sighed. It was no use. There just wasn't enough time. She might as well give up.

Mr. Stewart gave his daughter a sympathetic look. "Now hang in there, honey. You'll get it," he said consolingly.

Miley shook her head. "No, I won't. The

biology midterm is tomorrow, and there are two hundred and six bones in the body!" Not knowing what else to do, she stood up and began to pace in front of the couch. "It's not like I can learn them like . . ." She searched for a comparison. ". . . some new Hannah dance!" She threw her arms into the air.

Mr. Stewart thought for a moment. "Yeah, you do pick up on those pretty fast," he agreed.

"Yeah," said Miley. "That's because it's fun. Trust me, biology ain't!"

"Isn't," corrected Mr. Stewart.

Miley sighed. "I'm getting a B in English, Dad, that's not the problem. The problem is my biology teacher doesn't stand in front of the class going . . ." She picked up her bio book and spontaneously began to put together a song-and-dance routine, pointing to the body parts as she named them: "Tibia, fibula, clavicle, rib; we call this the humerus, and that's no fib!" She stopped and sighed. "Why can't it be that easy?"

"Good question," said Mr. Stewart. They stood there sadly, then realization dawned on both their faces at the same time. It *was* that easy—Miley just had to sing and dance it, and it would be a snap! They turned to each other.

"I thought of it first!" they both shouted.

"No, you didn't!" they said together again.

"Yes, I did," said Mr. Stewart.

"Didn't," argued Miley.

"Did," said Mr. Stewart.

"Didn't," retorted Miley.

"Did," said Mr. Stewart.

"Yes he did. Yes he did," squawked Snowball, jumping to Mr. Stewart's defense.

Mr. Stewart smiled and crossed his arms. "Like I said—love that bird."

Chapter Five

The next day at school, Oliver and Lilly watched openmouthed as Miley took them through her study-dance routine, set to the tune of Hannah Montana's hit song "Nobody's Perfect." She finished with the following lines:

"And now I take it home,
With the parietal bone.
It might be crazy.

But I learn that way!
Temporal and frontal, too.
And now I'm finally through.
That makes two hundred six.
I found a way that clicks!"

As Miley finished, she looked at her friends for their reaction.

"We're going to England. We're going to France," sang Lilly.

"We're going to Europe." Oliver joined in. *"'Cause she learned how to . . ."* He wasn't quite sure how to finish. *". . . memorize all the stuff."* He and Lilly folded their arms, and they each crossed one leg over the other. "Word!" they said together.

Miley smiled. She was ready to ace the test.

Meanwhile, Jackson had had enough of Snowball. He brought the bird to school with him, intending to give it back to Thor. He carried the cage into the quad and sat it down on a bench.

"Bodacious Becky, Bodacious Becky, Bodacious Becky," the parrot chanted.

Jackson sighed. "This is exactly why you're going back to Thor, you stupid birdbrain!" he said.

Ms. Kunkle walked by, looking through the stack of biology midterms she was about to pass out to Miley's class. "Morning, Stewart," she said to Jackson.

"Stupid birdbrain," replied Snowball.

Ms. Kunkle didn't even look up. "Detention, Stewart" she said.

"But it wasn't me," Jackson protested. He pointed to the cage to show Ms. Kunkle who was really to blame, but she was already gone. Jackson turned to Snowball. Enough was enough. "You know what?" he said angrily. "Why don't you just drop dead?"

And just like that, Snowball whimpered and toppled off his perch, deader than a doornail.

Jackson stared at the bird in disbelief. "Oh, no. What am I going to do?" he moaned. He gently took Snowball out of his cage. "Come on, buddy, speak to me. Say something. Anything!" he begged. He tried to think of something for Snowball to say. "Uh, uh, uh . . . 'Becky has bad breath?'" he suggested.

As luck would have it, that's just when Becky walked by. She stared at Jackson in disbelief. "I was gonna give you another chance, you jerk!" she cried. She whacked him in the shoulder with her book bag. That hurt! He dropped Snowball.

"Oh, no!" cried Jackson. "Wake up!" He fell to his knees. "Come back to me! Don't fly into the light!" As Jackson attempted to give the bird mouth-to-mouth resuscitation, Thor walked up to him, cheerful and clueless. He was wearing a sweatshirt that said I ♥ CHEESE. It seemed you could take the boy out of the Midwest, but you couldn't take the Midwest out of the boy!

"Hey, buddy," Thor said. "What's uh, Snowball's cage doing here?"

Jackson quickly hid Snowball inside his jacket, then turned to face Thor.

"Oh," Jackson said. "I brought him to school because I . . ." He had to think fast. "I've just grown so fond of him," he finished lamely.

"Oh," said Thor. He pointed to Jackson's chest. "You got him in there?"

"Yeah," Jackson said. "Because he was cold."

"Hey," Thor said to Snowball. "How you doing in there, buddy?"

Jackson poked Snowball's head out and imitated the bird's voice. "Great. Bye," he said tersely. He pushed Snowball's head back down inside his jacket. Thor looked at Jackson suspiciously, then reached inside the boy's jacket and took Snowball out. He cradled the bird in his arms like a little baby.

Jackson had no choice but to confess. "Okay," he began. "I was going to bring him back to you because he ruined my date and got me detention, but then I yelled at him and the next thing I knew it was 'bye-bye, birdie.'"

He waited for Thor to freak out. But instead Thor looked down at the bird and began to talk in baby talk. "You're playing dead again, aren't you? Aren't you, you silly little bird?"

Jackson's eyes nearly popped out of his head as Snowball sat up and perched on

Thor's shoulder. "Ta-da!" the bird squawked.

"Sweet niblets!" said Jackson. "I've been punk'd by a parrot!"

"Who does Daddy love?" Thor cooed.

"Snowball!" replied Snowball.

It was midterm time. Miley took a deep breath. She swiveled her neck and stretched her arms in preparation. She had her study song in her head and was raring to go. Next stop: Paris, France!

"All right class," announced Ms. Kunkle. "Eyes on your own paper. No talking. Oken?" she said.

"Yes, ma'am," replied Oliver.

"I said no talking!" the teacher snapped. "You have forty-five minutes. Good luck, everyone."

"Done," said Rico, seconds later. He stood up and headed toward Ms. Kunkle's desk. "Here you go, teach. Sorry it took so long, but I wanted to double-check my answers." He handed in his test, then walked smugly toward Miley. "Don't worry lollipop. You can always marry money," he said with a condescending smile.

Miley stuck out her tongue, and then Lilly stuck out her leg, tripping the Teeny-weeny Meanie. He went sprawling. Oops! Miley and Lilly gave each other a covert low five in celebration.

Okay, here we go, Miley thought. Question number one: name the three bones that make up the arm. All right, that's the humerus, the radius, and the . . . um, no . . . Miley scrunched her face, deep in thought. Hey, no problem. Just dance it out, she reminded herself. Miley began to dance in her seat and sing in her head:

When I milk the cow
On Uncle Earl's farm,
I use the ulna bone.
That is in my arm!

She threw her arms in the air.

Ulna! That was it! Miley quickly wrote the answer down. "Moo-ya!" she said out loud without thinking.

Ms. Kunkle walked over to Miley's desk. "Stewart, are you sending signals?" she asked suspiciously. "I won't have cheating in my class!"

"I'm not cheating," explained Miley. "Really, I'm just taking the test."

"Well then do it without all this," said Ms. Kunkle, imitating Miley by waving her arms around in the air.

"But I—" Miley started.

"—would be glad to Ms. Kunkle," the

teacher said, finishing the thought for her. "Took the words right out of your mouth, didn't I?"

Miley sighed. "Yes ma'am, yanked them out like a hungry raccoon in a doughnut-shop Dumpster," she said resignedly.

Ms. Kunkle wrinkled her nose. "A lot of people must find those country sayings charming," she said.

Miley grinned.

"I'm from Detroit," Ms. Kunkle continued. "We don't find anything charming. Now sit still."

Miley's smile faded.

Ms. Kunkle headed back to the front of the room. While the teacher's back was turned, Miley quickly looked at the next question and tried to dance the answer. But Ms. Kunkle turned around before Miley was done. Immediately, Miley froze with her arm straight up in the air. Thinking fast, she disguised her dance move as an underarm scratch.

But Ms. Kunkle wasn't buying it. She reached into one of her desk drawers and took out a pair of binoculars. She put them to her face and trained them directly on Miley. She was going to watch Miley's every move.

Miley gave her teacher a halfhearted wave. She was busted. Ms. Kunkle waved right back at her.

"I'm dead," said Miley.

Rico studied the chessboard, smiled, and moved one of the pieces. "There," he said, obviously pleased with his move. "See what you can do about that." He swiveled the board around and stared at the pieces. He was playing himself! "Ah, the Karkovski Entrapment," he said. "Clever, Rico. But not clever enough when you are dealing with *Rico*." He laughed menacingly.

Miley raised her hand. "Ms. Kunkle?" she said. "Can you ask the Rico twins to be quiet?" She held her test up. "Some of us are still trying to finish our test."

"Actually, Stewart," said Rico, "it's only you."

Miley looked around. Rico was right. Her classmates were reading magazines, filing their nails . . . Oliver was even playing with a Slinky.

Ms. Kunkle was of no help. "You have two minutes left," she told Miley. "No pressure. One-fifty-eight. Tick-tock, tick-tock," she added, bobbing her head back and forth.

"Thank you," said Miley with a fake smile.

Ms. Kunkle picked up an issue of *Cheap*

and Cheerful magazine and began to flip through it. Miley looked over at Lilly, shook her head in misery, and mouthed the word "help."

Lilly spoke softly to Oliver. "She can't do it without dancing," she explained. "We have to distract Kunkle."

Oliver grinned and held up a couple of packets of ketchup. "I'm way ahead of you," he answered. "You want 'paper cut,' 'bit my tongue,' or 'nosebleed'?"

Lilly's eyes lit up. "Ooh, nosebleed is my favorite!" she exclaimed.

"Then lean back, you're in the splashing zone," said Oliver, opening a packet and dribbling the contents under his nose. "Oh, man, it's a nosebleed!" he shouted.

"It's a gusher!" Lilly cried as a spray of ketchup shot out from between Oliver's fingers.

"It's a gusher, that's what it is," repeated Oliver. "Look everyone, it's a gusher!"

Ms. Kunkle grimaced and made her way to Oliver holding a box of tissues. Lilly seized the moment to gesture to Miley to start her desk-dance. Relieved, Miley immediately began dancing and filling in answers.

"Oken, honestly," said Ms. Kunkle, giving him a handful of tissues. "Paper cuts, bitten tongues, and now nosebleeds . . . we should put you in a helmet."

Meanwhile, Miley kept singing in her head and dancing in her seat.

With the parietal bone.
It might be crazy . . .

Ms. Kunkle chose that moment to turn around—just in time to see Miley doing a kick in her chair.

"Leg cramp!" explained Miley. "Just need to shake it off . . . with some dance steps?" she said unconvincingly. She held her knee and swung her leg back and forth.

Ms. Kunkle had had enough. "That's it, Stewart!" she snapped. "I warned you about cheating. Your test is over."

Miley's face fell. "But I'm not cheating!" she cried. "I know the answers, and I can prove it if I can move it!"

But Ms. Kunkle was not listening. She picked up Miley's test. "I suggest you 'move it' to the principal's office," she said. "Just go down the hall, make a left, then a right. When you see your brother, you're there."

Defeated, Miley got up and started for the door. But then she stopped. She wasn't going down without a fight. She had worked too hard for that! She spun around, took a deep breath, and began to sing and dance.

"Everybody knows the bones,
Just had to find a way.
Everybody knows what . . . what I'm talking
    about.
This is how I'll get an A."

Ms. Kunkle was exasperated. "Stewart, I thought I told you to—"

Lilly stood up. "Just give her a chance," she said. "Please," she added.

Miley continued to sing:

"My body has many parts,
And this is where it starts:
Phalanges, I have ten
And metatarsals, then.
I got some tarsals, too,
I put them in my shoe!"

Miley put her foot on a nearby desk.

Oliver stood up. "She's telling the truth," he said. He was still working the nosebleed, so his nose was pinched between his fingers. His voice came out all squeaky.

Miley continued to sing and dance.

"The fibula is next,
According to my text.
Then comes the tibia,
That ain't no fib-ia.
And now I'm up to the knee, yeah, yeah, yeah.
That's the patella to me."

By this time, Miley had danced her way to the front of the classroom. She leaned on a classmate's shoulder.

Lilly joined in, singing and dancing with her friend.

"Doin' the bone dance.
Study the answers
Again and again till I get it right."

Oliver gave up on the nosebleed and started dancing with his friends.

"Doin' the bone dance.
Ya dance and ya learn it.
And we won't mess up this test,
We'll get it perfect."

"C'mon, everybody!" Miley shouted to her classmates. "Move those fem—" she paused for a moment. "Femurs!" she said triumphantly.

Ms. Kunkle watched curiously, her arms crossed in front of her.

Rico walked over to the teacher's desk and started flipping through the test papers. "Yeah, by the look of these tests, you losers need all the help you can get," he said with a snicker.

Some of Miley's classmates joined in and they all danced down the aisle.

> *"Doin' the bone dance.*
> *Ya dance and ya learn it.*
> *And we won't mess up this test,*
> *We'll get it perfect . . . word."*

The next thing Miley knew, the desks had been shoved aside, and the whole class was singing and dancing.

> *"Doin' the bone dance.*
> *Study the answers*
> *Again and again till I get it right.*
> *Doin' the bone dance.*
> *Ya dance and ya learn it.*
> *And we won't mess up this test,*
> *We'll get it perfect . . ."*

Just then, the bell rang. Biology class was over. The students all cheered and began to file out of the classroom.

"That's it, Stewart," said Ms. Kunkle. "I'm going to the principal."

Miley couldn't believe her ears "What?" she cried.

Ms. Kunkle smiled. "I want you to show him that dance. It's the best study technique I've ever seen." She began to sing: *"By the way, you got an A. Word!"*

She danced her way out the classroom door.

Miley, Oliver, and Lilly turned to each other, their mouths open in shock. "We're going to Europe!" they shouted.

"Gimme a little metacarpal love!" exclaimed Miley. They all high-fived each other.

As they happily gathered their things,

Rico came back into the classroom. He stood there silently, staring at Miley, his hand to his chin. He was deep in thought.

"What?" asked Miley.

"That song," said Rico, his eyes narrowed. "Your voice. Those moves. It all reminds me of some famous singer."

Miley, Lilly, and Oliver looked at each other in a panic. They had to think fast! Rico could never know Miley's secret. They knew the Evil Little Boy would blackmail her with it, and her life would be a living nightmare!

"Kelly Clarkson?" suggested Miley hopefully.

"Hilary Duff?" said Lilly.

"Jay-Z?" Oliver put in. Everyone looked at him. He shrugged his shoulders. He wasn't good under pressure!

"I got it!" Rico cried. "Hannah Montana!"

The three friends froze for an instant, then threw their heads back in laughter.

"Hannah Montana," said Miley. "You old joker, you!"

Rico smiled, then shook his head. "You're right, what was I thinking? This bubble brain could never pull off something like that," he said, pointing at Miley.

"Yeah, what were you thinking?" said Oliver. "We're talking nothin' upstairs. If you know what I mean."

To demonstrate, Lilly pulled back Miley's hair and pretended she could look into her ear and see straight through to the other side. "Hey Oliver, I can see you!" she said.

Oliver looked into Miley's other ear. "Hey!" he said back to Lilly.

"Hey!" said Lilly. They waved to each other.

Part One

"London, England; Paris, France," **Miley sang.** *"Watch me do my Europe dance!"*

Miley's eyes flew open as she realized that the Stewart who was in trouble this time was *her*.

"Come on, Rico. I've been standing like this for two hours," Miley complained.

"I needed someone to hold the globe," Rico told Miley.

"We're going to Europe 'cause she learned how to . . .
memorize all the stuff," Oliver sang.

Thinking fast, Miley disguised her dance move as
an underarm scratch.

Miley gave her teacher a halfhearted wave. She was busted.

Miley and Lilly had to think fast. Rico could never know Miley's secret!

Part Two

Mikayla and Hannah Montana gave each other a huge fake hug for the camera. May the best pop star win!

"Don't come crying when I break your little rubber-band toy," Mr. Stewart said mockingly.

Miley was worried. If Lilly was right, her dad's back
wouldn't be better in time to go to Florida!

Miley and Lilly stared at each other, shocked at
hearing Mikayla's insult.

"I was just making sure all the carry-ons were stowed properly," Miley said to Suzy the stewardess.

"Hey, this bathroom's *occupado*," Miley said, trying to disguise herself.

"Darlin', no dad wants to see his little girl grow up,
but every dad knows someday she has to,"
Mr. Stewart said.

"Lilly and I just watched the concert on TV,"
Mr. Stewart said, lying upside down on an inversion
table. "You were terrific!"

Miley rolled her eyes. The lengths she went to, the humiliation she had to suffer to keep her identity a secret! But at least she was going to Europe. And she earned it all by herself. By figuring out a really creative way to learn. By working hard and not being discouraged. By *doin' the bone dance. Word!*

PART TWO

Chapter One

Miley Stewart—dressed as Hannah Montana in a long, blond wig, a shiny turquoise jacket, and white jeans—was a guest on the popular talk show *The Real Deal with Collin Lasseter*. She and Collin, an older man in a suit and glasses, watched as Mikayla, a rising young pop star, performed her new hit song, "If Cupid Had a Heart."

Miley and Collin applauded enthusiastically as Mikayla, wearing a red hat, lace shirt, denim jacket, and white skirt, finished her song and walked over to take her place next to Miley. Miley thought Mikayla had done a really great job. She impulsively jumped up and gave the girl a big hug. Miley knew what it was like to be starting out in the business and how important it was to have support.

Collin spoke into the camera. "That was Mikayla's 'If Cupid Had a Heart,' her first top-ten hit." He smiled at the young singer. "All you need now is another *dozen* to match the record of Hannah Montana." He turned to Miley. "What do you think, Hannah? Has she got the right stuff?"

"Totally, Collin," Miley answered sincerely. "I think she's great."

"Thanks Hannah," replied Mikayla. "That means a lot coming from you."

"I'm welling up at the love and respect I

feel between these two princesses of pop," Collin said.

Miley grinned. "Well, I think there's enough room in the music world for both of us, right Mikayla?" She reached forward and touched Mikayla's hand.

"Absotively posilutely!" Mikayla replied cheerfully.

Collin chuckled. "Adorable. You're not going to want to miss these two sharing the stage next week at the United People's Relief Charity concert in Florida. We'll be right back." He paused, took off his glasses, and addressed the camera. "I'm Collin Lasseter, and this is *The Real Deal*."

"And we're out," said the stage manager. It was time for commercials.

Collin immediately stood up. "Speaking of relief, I've got the bladder of a kitten." He laughed embarrassedly and made a beeline for the bathroom.

Smiling, Miley turned to Mikayla, who was playing with the magenta ends of her long, dark hair. "It's truly great to finally meet you," Miley said sincerely. She put her hand to her chest. "I really am a huge fan," she confessed.

Mikayla smiled pleasantly, and then said, quite unexpectedly, "Yeah, I hate you."

"Thanks, I feel the exact same way," said Miley. Suddenly Mikayla's words sank in. Miley looked puzzled. Had she heard the girl correctly? "What?"

Mikayla stood up and began to list the reasons she was not Hannah Montana's greatest fan. "Your voice is stenchy, your music is stupid, and your outfits make me want to puke on them—but it looks like someone already did." She crossed the room to pick up a bottle of water. Miley followed her, determined to be gracious. "Okay," she said. "I don't know what your problem is, but—"

Mikayla wouldn't let her finish. "My problem is, I'm ten times better than you, and you're going to find that out in Florida, Miss Hannah-I'm-Takin'-All-Your-Fannahs," she said, shaking her finger in Miley's face and doing the head-bob thing.

Miley had had enough. It was time for the gloves to come off. "Okay, listen here, you one-hit bobblehead, the only thing you're takin' from me is lessons. Okay, lesson number one: *this* is how you do the head-bob thing," she said, demonstrating the proper technique.

Mikayla stared at her.

"That's right," said Miley, touching Mikayla's red hat. "I went there."

Mikayla leaned in close to Miley. "Well,

you know where I'm gonna go?" she said.

Miley folded her arms across her chest. "Down the toilet with the rest of your career?" she said cheerfully. "That's right, I went there again. And this time I brought property." She turned her back on Mikayla.

Just then, Margot, Mikayla's no-nonsense manager, rushed on to the set. "Back up, kid," she said as she pushed Mikayla out of her way. Miley could see where Mikayla got her bad attitude from. This woman was obnoxious! Margot got right into Miley's face. "And don't go shootin' off your little teenybopper mouth at my client."

"She started it," said Miley.

"And I'm ending it," said Margot. She leaned in close to Miley. "Little Miss Soon-to-Be-Used-to-Be."

Just then Miley's dad, Mr. Stewart, arrived, wearing his manager's disguise. He had heard everything that Margot had said. "Whoa, Nellie, I don't know who put the burr underneath your saddle, but no one talks to *my* client that way," he said.

"It's okay. I can handle it," Miley told him.

"You heard her, Zeke," said Margot. "Why don't you go outside and wait in your wagon?"

"Excuse me?" said Mr. Stewart.

Margot stepped closer and took a close look at his fake mustache. "And while you're at it, you might want to shave that ferret off your face, okay?"

Mr. Stewart leaned forward. "I'll shave mine when you shave yours," he said.

Margot gasped.

"That's right, I went there," said Mr. Stewart.

The stage manager broke the tension.

"We're back in five, four, three . . ." he announced.

The two girls scrambled to their seats, fake smiles plastered across their faces. Collin rushed in, plopping down in his chair just as the cameras began to roll.

Collin gave a hearty laugh. "Great story, Hannah. Hey, we're back and we're having some fun now, aren't we, girls?"

Mikayla smiled. "Oh, yeah, I just can't wait till Florida."

Miley gave an even bigger grin. "Neither can I."

The two girls gave each other a huge fake hug for the camera, their heads pressed together as if they were the best of friends. But both Miley and Mikayla knew this wasn't over—the next round would take place on the stage in Florida. And may the best pop star win!

Chapter Two

The next day, Miley was Miley again. Back to her everyday appearance, she wore a green knit sleeveless dress over a white T-shirt and skinny jeans; a green plaid headband was in her long, brown hair. She was with Lilly, who had her hair in a ponytail with black and pink ribbons woven into her hair. She wore a pink waffle thermal top and long shorts.

Miley and Lilly walked in the front door

to find Mr. Stewart eating his lunch—a sandwich and a bag of chips—as he talked on the phone.

Miley was still fuming over the incident with Mikayla. "I can't wait to get to that concert and show that two-faced, tone-deaf toad who's boss," Miley told Lilly. She raised her arms, her hands balled up into fists.

"Yeah, but you have to wear something amazing," Lilly reminded her. "Mikayla always looks incredible."

The last thing Miley wanted to hear at that moment was about the excellent fashion sense of her brand-new worst enemy. She gave Lilly a look.

Lilly knew it was time to backtrack. "For a two-faced, tone-deaf toad," she added with a squeak.

Miley and Lilly walked toward Mr. Stewart to see what he was up to.

"Well I don't care what Mikayla wants," Mr. Stewart said into the phone. He was talking to Margot, who had called from the recording studio. "It's a benefit concert, and all the girls are sharing one dressing room."

Mr. Stewart was putting Mikayla and her manager into their place! The two girls liked the sound of that. Miley and Lilly began to dance. "Go, Daddy! Go, Daddy!" Miley sang.

"I don't think so," Margot retorted. "Unlike you and your 'kinfolk,' my client didn't grow up in a barn, and we're expecting our own dressing room."

"I can see why you would need more room," Mr. Stewart replied. "I mean, where else are you gonna put Mikayla's ego and your big mouth?"

"Step off, goober," Margot said menacingly.

Mr. Stewart was done talking. He picked up his bag of chips and crushed it into the receiver. "Oh, dear, I'm afraid I'm losin' ya," he said. "You're breaking up."

But Margot was on to him. "I know that trick," she said. "You're crunching potato chips."

"They're corn chips," Mr. Stewart corrected her. "And you're not getting another room!" He hung up the phone, then picked up his sandwich and sat down at the table.

"And that's the way Robby Ray rolls," he said. Miley and Lilly followed Mr. Stewart and stood on either side of him.

"Could Robby Ray roll out some cash?" Miley asked hopefully. "Hannah needs a new outfit for Florida." She had to look amazing in Florida—she just had to!

"I thought you were gonna wear that snazzy silver dress," said Mr. Stewart.

Miley rolled her eyes. "Dad, please get with the times; that is so yesterday."

Mr. Stewart was exasperated. "That's because yesterday's the day you bought it!" he exclaimed.

"Ooh!" exclaimed Lilly. She began to speak in best-friend shorthand. "What about the one you bought at the place next to the place we went that one time?"

Miley made a face. "No that one's too . . ." she flipped her hand back and forth.

"Yeah, you're right," Lilly agreed. "Plus when you wear that, you have to wear . . ."

"I know," Miley said. "And I hate those."

"Who doesn't?" agreed Lilly.

"What about the one I bought after the one I bought at the place next to the place?" Miley suggested.

Lilly was delighted. "The one that goes with the shoes with the things? I love that one!" she squealed.

"Me, too," said Mr. Stewart cheerfully.

The girls stared at him.

"Do you even know what we're talking about?" Miley asked.

"No," Mr. Stewart replied. "But as long as it doesn't cost me a wad of cash, I'm all for it." He clapped his hands and rubbed them together.

Miley rolled her eyes.

"Your dad . . ." said Lilly.

"I know," replied Miley.

Mr. Stewart shook his head. Daughters! Then he heard a strange noise coming from the deck. Weird. It sounded like— grunting. He stood up from the table and made his way outside. And that's where he found Jackson, working out on a big exercise machine—his brand-new Solo-Bend-A-Flex 5000. Jackson was making funny faces as he strained to work his arms.

"Push . . . push . . . push," Jackson chanted.

"Son, are you working out on that contraption or giving birth to it?" Mr. Stewart asked, trying to keep a straight face.

Jackson scowled. "Laugh all you want, old man," he said. "But when the guns come in, there's gonna be"—he flexed one bicep—"a new sheriff in town." He flexed the other. "And a new deputy. Bang!"

"When I was a kid, we didn't have money for this kind of stuff," Mr. Stewart told his son. "You know what we lifted? Cows. And when it rained, we went inside and lifted your Aunt Pearl. Try lifting her after a bowl of her homemade pinto-bean soup." He flexed his own biceps. "Talk about your bang, pow!"

Jackson couldn't believe his ears. "Are

you saying this isn't a workout?" he asked in disbelief.

"I'm not saying that at all," Mr. Stewart said, running his hand through his hair. "I'm thinking it, but I'm not saying it," he added with a grin.

Those were fighting words! "All right, well, I'd like to see you give it a try, Flabio," replied Jackson. He got up off the machine so his dad could take a seat at the Solo-Bend-A-Flex 5000.

Mr. Stewart sat down. "Okay, but don't come crying when I break your little rubber-band toy," he said mockingly. He grabbed the arm attachments and let out a loud "Ugggggh." Then he began working his arms with ease. "You know I'm just kiddin' ya, right?"

"It wasn't set for your height and weight," Jackson explained defensively.

"Fine," said Mr. Stewart. "Then set it for my height and weight. Crank it up to 'Aunt Pearl,'" he suggested.

Jackson began spinning the adjustment wheel to give his dad the proper workout. Perhaps he adjusted it a bit too tightly. . . .

"I'd like to see the rubber-band toy that could handle Robby Raaaaaaaay!" Suddenly, before Jackson's unbelieving eyes, Mr. Stewart was flung off of the machine and over the deck rail. He landed with a loud thud in the sand.

Jackson's mouth fell open in disbelief. He vaulted himself over the deck after his dad.

Sweet niblets—Jackson was going to be in trouble now!

Chapter Three

Miley came bouncing down the stairs in a fabulous Hannah ensemble. Lilly was right behind her. Miley was wearing the outfit she bought after the one she bought at the place next to the place, the one that went with the shoes with the things—a silky red dress with a white print and a handkerchief hem. She wore it over a white tank and skinny jeans, with silver heels and several necklaces. "Hey Dad, this is the dress I'm gonna . . ." She cut herself short as she realized that Jackson was leading the groaning Mr. Stewart into the living room. "What happened?" she asked.

Jackson put on his best Arnold Schwarzenegger accent. "Mr. Puny-verse just got a butt-whooping from an itsy-bitsy, teeny-weeny, little bitty rubber band," he explained.

The girls were shocked—Mr. Stewart looked positively awful.

Mr. Stewart groaned. "Boy, I'm going to get to feeling better soon," he said to Jackson, "and when I do, I am coming after you."

"Oh, no, I better run!' Jackson scoffed, pretending to be scared. He began to move away from his dad in super–slo-mo as Mr. Stewart tried to grab him. Mr. Stewart gave up and grabbed his own back instead.

"You look terrible," said Lilly. "Are you

going to be able to make it to Florida?"

"Lilly," Miley scolded, "he's obviously in pain. We have to show a little concern." She turned to her father. "Daddy, can I get you an ice pack?" she asked in an overly concerned voice. "A pillow?" She paused, then got right down to business. "Are you going to be able to make it to Florida?"

"Don't worry about me, honey," said Mr. Stewart. "I'm gonna be fine."

Miley was relieved, but only for an instant.

"I doubt it!" Lilly exclaimed. Miley turned to her, a quizzical expression on her face. "When my dad's back goes out, he can't move for days. He just sleeps on the dining-room table. Last Thanksgiving we had to eat around him. He had a muscle spasm—giblets everywhere!"

Was Lilly right? Was Miley's dad down for the count? Miley turned to her dad to see him topple onto the couch with a loud "Ugh." Things were not looking very promising for the Florida trip. Not one bit.

When the going got tough, Miley called on her bodyguard, Roxy DeLizes, a former U.S. Marine. The two had met when Miley's dad took her to buy her very first Hannah Montana wig. Roxy had been a security guard at the store and helped Miley make her choice. She'd been Miley's right-hand woman ever since. Miley, Roxy, and Lilly stood in the living room together.

"Roxy, this treatment better work, or I can kiss Florida good-bye," Miley said worriedly.

"Oh, no problem girl," replied Roxy. "There's never been a jacked-up back that Roxy couldn't crack," she said confidently.

"You know, I'm feeling better already," Mr. Stewart said nervously. He was strapped to a large table and was hanging upside down. "I think this treatment's doing the trick."

"Oh, that's not the treatment," Roxy said with a laugh. "This is," she added, giving the table a spin. Mr. Stewart began to rotate faster and faster.

Miley stared, openmouthed, as her dad spun around like a chicken on a hyperfast spit. Then she grimaced as she heard a cracking noise.

"Ah, ah, ah!" yelled Mr. Stewart.

"Oh, no," said Miley. "I think the machine broke."

"That . . . wasn't . . . the . . . machine!" Mr. Stewart managed to shout.

Miley gulped. She sure hoped Roxy knew what she was doing!

"Daddy, I am so sorry," Miley said to her dad as she walked through the front door on their way back from the emergency room. "I was just trying to help."

Mr. Stewart, held up by Jackson, hobbled in next. He wore a back brace, with a head strap and a chin rest. Things had gone from bad to worse.

"It's okay Mile," he told her. "I know you had your heart set on putting that Mikayla in her place, but there's no way I'm going to be able to sit on a plane for five hours."

Miley's heart sank. Jackson helped his dad to the couch, and Miley sat down next to him. She was defeated. "I guess you're right," she agreed. "Unless we strap you to a surfboard and check you through luggage!" she added, half-kidding, half-serious.

"Why don't you just stick him in a

coffin?" suggested Jackson sarcastically. "At least they're padded."

But Miley took him seriously. "That's a great idea!" she exclaimed. "We could get him a little portable DVD player. Time would just fly by!"

It was all too much for Mr. Stewart. He toppled over onto his side, and Miley and Jackson lifted him back up by one of his arms. "Ain't gonna happen," Mr. Stewart said, once he was upright. "Let's face it, you tried, Roxy tried."

A light went off in Miley's head. "Roxy!" she exclaimed. "That's a great idea! Daddy, Roxy could take me!"

Miley threw her arms around her dad. He groaned in pain.

"No, no, no way, honey," Mr. Stewart said.

"Why not?" Miley wanted to know.

"Roxy's taken me to plenty of concerts before." It made perfect sense. She didn't know why her dad was fighting it.

"Not all the way across the country," Mr. Stewart argued. "Besides, let's face it, if I'm not there with you, Mikayla's manager's gonna steamroll right over you." He hated the thought of not being there to protect his daughter.

"Oh, come on, Dad," said Miley. "I can handle Mikayla *and* her manager." She stood up. "And I'll have Roxy. Remember? Roxy like a puma!" Miley extended her left hand like a paw and swiped the air, Roxy's signature move.

"Honey we can't," said Mr. Stewart. "You're just a kid."

Miley's voice began to rise. Why was her dad treating her like a child? "But I'm *your* kid, and you taught me how to stand up and fight for myself. And I'll have Roxy. Face it, Dad, it's all falling into place."

Mr. Stewart began to tilt to the right. Jackson grabbed him. "Not for me it isn't," Mr. Stewart said. This was too much for him to take—Miley's sudden independence, his aching back. It was all happening too fast.

"Why not?" said Miley, her voice rising. "You know I can do this. You can trust me," she added.

"But that's not the point," argued Mr. Stewart.

"Then what is the point?" Miley demanded.

"The point is, you're not ready to do this on your own," said Mr. Stewart.

"Yes I am, Daddy, and you know it!" Miley sat next to him on the couch. "Come on Dad, let me go, please," she begged.

Mr. Stewart was done arguing. "That's

it, Mile. I don't want to talk about this anymore."

"That's not fair!" Miley cried.

"I don't have to be fair," retorted Mr. Stewart, falling back on the oldest dad argument in the book. "I'm the dad, and I'm not letting you go."

Miley stood up. "Why are you treating me like such a baby?" she shouted.

"Because you're acting like one!" Mr. Stewart replied.

"But Dad—" Miley started.

"No, Miley! Not another word!" he said, pointing to her.

"Fine," said Miley bitterly. "How about three?" She crossed her arms. "I hate you!" she shouted, bursting into tears. She turned around and ran upstairs to her room. She couldn't believe she just said that to her dad. But she knew she was right. She knew she was ready for this. And he *was* treating her like a baby! It was so unfair!

Mr. Stewart struggled to stand. "Miley, Miley Ray!" he called. Then he tilted over and fell facedown onto the couch.

Jackson saw his chance and ran with it. "Does this mean I'm your favorite kid now?" he asked hopefully.

"Erfmmuph," Mr. Stewart said, muffled by the pillow.

That was enough for Jackson. "I'll take that as a 'yes,'" he said, satisfied. He slapped his dad on the butt.

Chapter Four

Later that day at Rico's Surf Shop, the beachfront store owned by Rico's father, Miley was still fuming. She paced back and forth as Lilly sat at a nearby table. "I've never said anything like that to my dad before," Miley said. "But he wasn't making any sense, and I got so mad and—uggggh, I hate him for making me say I hate him!" She sat down and slapped the round, blue picnic table to emphasize her point.

"This is terrible," Lilly said with a sigh. "Now Mikayla's going to have that stage all to herself." Once again, Lilly had chosen the exact wrong thing to say.

Miley stared at her friend. "Lilly, I'm upset enough. The last thing I want to think about is—"

"Mikayla!" a radio announcer's voice boomed. "Comin' at you with her new hit single, 'If Cupid Had a Heart.'" The dreaded song began to play.

Miley spun around. The music was coming from the tiki hut, where Rico was listening to a boom box. He turned up the volume and started moving to the music.

"Rico, would you turn that down?" Miley asked.

"I'm sorry," said Rico in a sincere tone. "Is it bothering you?"

"Yeah!" said Miley.

"Well, this will drive you crazy." Rico turned up the volume and began singing along with the music. Then he jumped onto the counter and began to dance under the funky, colorful lights that hung overhead. Miley glared at him, then noticed a rubber football lying nearby in the sand. She picked it up and turned toward Rico with a devilish smile. Ready, aim, fire—her aim was true. She hit Rico right in the stomach, and he and his boom box fell off the counter. Miley grinned. The Mikayla show was over.

Miley looked satisfied for a moment. But then her cell phone rang. She looked at the caller ID. "Ugh," she said with a grimace. "Speak of the she-devil." She opened her phone. "What is it, Mikayla?" she snapped. Lilly leaned over to listen in.

Mikayla sat on a stool in a recording

studio, wearing a purple shirt with hot pink armbands around her biceps. Her hair was crimped perfectly and she had headphones around her neck. "Hannah I just heard you pulled out of the concert. What happened?" she asked in mock sympathy. Then she dropped the concerned act and returned to her regular unpleasant personality. "Did the pop star get scared?" she asked in a baby voice.

Miley had had enough. "Listen Mikcockroach," she snapped. "One of my family members has a *serious* medical condition, okay."

Mikayla rolled her eyes. "Yeah, and it's called 'wimpatitus,'" she said. "That means you're a wimp," she explained, unnecessarily.

"I know what it means!" spluttered Miley, switching the phone to her other ear. Lilly scrambled to change sides, too.

"Oh, I can see the headlines now," said Mikayla. "'Mikayla Rocks While Heartless Hannah Hides from the Homeless.'"

Classic Mikayla! "The concert's for *hunger* relief!" said Miley disgustedly.

Lilly made a face.

"Like I care," said Mikayla dismissively. "Either way, I'm gonna steal all your fans, and there's nothing you can do about it."

"Oh, yes there is!" Miley cried. She switched ears again, and Lilly changed positions, too. "I am gonna be there."

"You are?" said Mikayla incredulously.

"You are?" whispered Lilly, looking shocked.

Miley turned to Lilly. "Yes," she said, holding the phone away from her ear. Then she spoke into the receiver. "And you better wear something absorbent, 'cause I'm gonna be wiping the stage with you.

That's right, I went there." She snapped the phone shut.

Lilly turned to Miley. "You can't go to Florida without your dad."

"Watch me," said Miley, walking away.

Lilly stared after Miley. "Wooooowwww," she said. Then she raced after her friend. This was getting serious! How was Miley going to pull this one off?

Chapter Five

Mr. Stewart sat at his desk in a checkered bathrobe, still wearing a back brace. He held a sheet of loose-leaf paper in his hand.

"*'By the time you read this,'*" he read, "*'Roxy and I will be on our way to Florida. And when I come back I'll take whatever punishment you decide to give me like the grown-up I'm trying* to convince you I am. P.S. Don't blame Roxy, she doesn't know.'"

Mr. Stewart couldn't believe what he had just read. Miley had never been so disobedient before! "Dangflabbit!" he shouted. "Jackson, get down here and help me out of this thing!" He reached up and pulled off the head strap. Jackson appeared as fast as he could, considering he was wearing a wet suit, the mask pulled up on his forehead. He automatically assumed the worst.

"Oh, come on, Dad, not another sponge bath," he said with a groan. "Haven't I done enough?"

Mr. Stewart slowly rose to his feet. "Not until you get me to the airport," he said.

Jackson started to head for the car, then turned around to face his dad. "Maybe we should change first," he suggested.

"Good idea," said Mr. Stewart. He

limped off upstairs. Miley had gone too far this time.

Miley and Roxy sat in the posh first-class cabin, luxuriating in the wide, comfy white leather seats. Actually, Roxy was the one who was enjoying herself. Miley just looked on edge as she waited for the plane to take off. Just then the captain's voice came over the intercom. "Sorry for the delay, folks. We'll be leaving the gate momentarily. Thank you for your patience."

"Mmm," said Roxy, totally content. "Warm cashews, cold shrimp, and . . ." She held up a pair of soft slippers. ". . . complimentary slippers. Time to let the dogs out."

"Great, glad you're enjoying the flight," Miley snapped sarcastically. "It'll be a whole lot better when we *take off*! Come on flyboy! I could walk to Florida faster than this!" she shouted, waving her arms. "Come on!"

One of the flight attendants, a chipper woman named Suzy, appeared, a huge smile plastered across her face. "Sweetheart, can you keep it down?" she said through her grin. "Someone just complained."

"Who?" Miley wanted to know.

Suzy's smile never faltered. "Me," she replied. "Now, zip it. Thank you," she concluded pleasantly.

Roxy, a leopard-print sleep mask on her face, was wearing her complimentary headphones as she happily pushed the buttons on her armrest to browse through the music-channel selections. She finally found one she liked.

"Ooh, channel twenty-one is all Barry White, all night!" she said. "Ooh, baby, baby," she added in a deep Barry White voice. She pulled the sleep mask down over her eyes and began grooving to the music.

Just then, the captain's voice came over the intercom again. "Flight attendants, please close the doors and prepare for take-off," he announced.

Whew. Miley was relieved. "Yes!" she cried happily.

Suddenly, Mr. Stewart poked his head through the curtain separating first class from the rest of the plane. Jackson was right behind him. They stopped and spoke to a male flight attendant. "Excuse me, I'm looking for my daughter," Mr. Stewart explained.

Miley heard her father's voice and froze, her eyes opened wide. "Sweet niblets," she said with a grimace. She turned around and peeked down the aisle. Luckily, the man behind her chose that moment to stand up and put something in the overhead compartment, which obstructed her dad's view. Miley got down on her hands and knees in her hot pink sweat suit and started making her way down the aisle in the opposite direction.

She stopped as she came face-to-knees with Suzy, who was standing in the middle of the aisle. Miley looked up to see the flight attendant's big, fake grin. Miley smiled back, just as big and just as fake. "I was just making sure all the carry-ons were stowed properly," Miley explained. "No need to thank me. She glanced at Suzy's footwear. "Sensible shoes," she noted. "Good choice." She gave Suzy a thumbs-up.

Suzy smiled another toothy grin. "I really don't like you. Please take your seat," she said, indicating the way with the flight-attendant, two-finger point directional. "Thank you," she concluded.

Miley climbed into the closest seat, in the center aisle next to an elderly woman eating shrimp cocktail. She sank into the seat, wondering what in the world she was going to do next.

Mr. Stewart and Jackson were still searching the first-class cabin for Miley.

"Miley!" called Jackson.

"Mile," said Mr. Stewart.

Miley looked over the seat wearing a borrowed grandma head-scarf and a pair of oversize sunglasses. "I was just visiting my grandkids in Palm Springs," she said to her seatmate in a raspy, old-lady voice. "And you?" The woman stared at Miley, totally confused.

Miley decided it was time to make her escape. Still in the head-scarf and sunglasses, she walked down the aisle to the back of the first-class section, passing her brother, who was searching through an overhead compartment. "Pardon me, doll-face," said Miley in her old-lady voice. "Gotta make a pit stop," she explained, ducking into a coat closet.

Just then, Jackson spotted Roxy in her window seat, grooving away to Barry White. "Roxy?" he said. When she didn't respond he tapped her on the shoulder to get her attention. "Roxy!"

Roxy, her eye mask still in place, snapped into bodyguard mode. "Hi-ya!" she shouted, grabbing Jackson and knocking him across the aisle into a seat. Luckily it was empty and right next to a pretty blond girl. Surprised, she turned to look at her new seatmate.

"Well, hello," said Jackson, making the best of the slightly awkward situation.

Realizing something strange was going on, Roxy removed her sleeping mask and looked around. She spotted Mr. Stewart in the aisle.

"Robby Ray, what are you doing here?" she asked. Suddenly she knew exactly what was happening. "Oh, no, she didn't!" she exclaimed.

"Oh, yes, she did," said Mr. Stewart, shaking his head. "She bamboozled us both."

"Yeah," said Roxy. "But your bam is easy to boozle. You still don't know I sneak over to your house and use your hot tub on the weekends."

"What?" said Mr. Stewart.

Oops! Roxy changed the subject immediately. "Enough of this chitchat," she said. "Let's find that girl." She walked down the aisle, Mr. Stewart limping behind her. She stopped in front of the coat closet and opened it. And there was Miley, still in the sunglasses and scarf, attempting to hide in the back.

"Hey, this bathroom is *occupado*," Miley said in the old-lady voice. She closed the curtain. Roxy opened it. In desperation, Miley switched to flight-attendant mode. "Sorry, doll-face, you know you really need to keep this closed. I may shift during flight."

She pulled the curtain shut. Roxy opened it again and gave Miley an irritated look.

"Oh, you're gonna shift right now," said Roxy. "Get out here."

Miley knew the jig was up. She got out.

"Get that thing off your head," said Mr. Stewart. "We're going home."

"But, Dad," protested Miley, taking off the scarf.

"No 'but.' Now," said Mr. Stewart. He

turned to the flight attendant, Suzy. "Excuse me, ma'am," he said pleasantly. "We'd like to get off."

Suzy smiled her big smile. "And I'd like to have a job where I didn't have to smile all the time no matter how annoyed I am. Now the doors are closed, and no one's getting off until our first stop in Denver. So please, take your seats."

"But we—" Mr. Stewart started to say.

"I said *please*!" Suzy squeaked.

Mr. Stewart paused for a moment, then turned to Miley. "Miley Stewart," he said. "I have never been so disappointed in you."

Suzy smiled. "You think you're disappointed now, wait till you see your snack box back in coach." Gently but quite firmly, she guided Mr. Stewart back to his assigned seat. As he passed by Jackson, still chatting away with his pretty blond seatmate, Mr. Stewart grabbed his son by the ear, and dragged him along. "Ow, ow, ow, ow, ow," said Jackson.

It was a different world back in coach. Jackson was squeezed into a dreaded middle seat, squashed between his dad and a large sleeping man in a blue Hawaiian shirt. To add insult to injury, a boy in the row behind them kept rhythmically kicking the back of Jackson's seat. Jackson turned around. "Listen kid . . ." he started to say.

Then he saw the kid's father. And changed his mind immediately.

"You've got a fantastic sense of rhythm," Jackson finished. "You must be very proud," he said, addressing the father. He quickly turned back around.

"Big dad?" asked Mr. Stewart.

"Huge. With a Mohawk," replied Jackson.

Just then his large seatmate snorted, groaned, and leaned his head on Jackson's shoulder. Jackson was fuming.

"See, why would I want to hang out with my friends when I can spend five hours being kicked in the back by the Kangaroo Kid and drooled on by Jabba the Gut?" he asked his father.

"Don't blame me, blame your sister," said Mr. Stewart grumpily.

"Why? You're the one who wouldn't let her go in the first place," Jackson argued.

"Don't start with me son," Mr. Stewart said defensively. "She wasn't ready to go."

"*She* wasn't ready, or you weren't?" Jackson asked pointedly.

Mr. Stewart couldn't believe his ears. "Excuse me?" he asked.

"Come on, Dad. I mean, you raised us to believe we could do anything we set our minds to. The whole time we were growing up you told us, 'I know you can do it, so get ready, get set, go.' Why aren't you saying that now?"

Mr. Stewart stared at Jackson.

"Oh, yeah, I can be deep," Jackson said.

As Mr. Stewart thought about what his son had just said, Jackson's large seatmate turned and put his arms around Jackson. Jackson looked at his dad, then rolled his eyes. Sometimes it didn't pay to be the brother of a teen pop star!

Roxy was still angry with Miley, but not upset enough to turn down one of Suzy's freshly baked chocolate chip cookies. Mmm, mmm, good!

"Roxy, I am really sorry that I lied to you," said Miley, biting her lip.

"Hush up, I'm not talking to you," replied Roxy dismissively. She paused. "But if I *was* talking to you, I'd be saying, 'Don't apologize to me, apologize to your daddy, because he only does what he does because he loves you.'"

Miley considered this. "I guess I should apologize, shouldn't I?" she asked.

"If I was talking to you, I'd say 'Mmm-hmmm,'" Roxy said.

Miley stood up as Roxy picked up her cookie. "I'd also say, 'While you're up, pick me up some two percent.'" She smiled and took a bite. "Roxy likes to dunk."

Miley was heading down the aisle when Mr. Stewart appeared through the curtain.

"I was just—" her dad began.

"Me, too," said Miley. "Dad, when I said that I hated you, I was just . . ."

"I know. Honey, sit down," he said,

pointing to two unoccupied seats in the center. "I think we need to talk."

Yikes. Just what Miley had feared. "Oh, man," she said. "I was hoping we'd just said it all."

Mr. Stewart smiled. "Not quite," he replied.

She sat, and Mr. Stewart gingerly lowered himself into the seat next to her with a groan.

"I think we both know what you did was wrong," Mr. Stewart began. "But we can talk about that later." He sighed. "Right now, I have something I want to give you."

He pulled out a motion-sickness bag and handed it to her.

"A barf bag?" said Miley, not quite believing her eyes. Was her dad losing it?

"It has a song on it," Mr. Stewart explained. "I just wrote it for you."

A song? Miley looked at her dad, surprised.

"I know you didn't understand why I was acting the way that I was. Well, I didn't understand it either," Mr. Stewart confessed. "I'm hoping that this will help explain."

Mr. Stewart began to sing. Miley looked down at the bag, following along with the lyrics. As he sang about not being ready to let his little girl grow up, Miley started to remember all the times her father had been there for her. She knew she'd never have been able to pull off her double life without his support.

Miley looked up and smiled as her dad finished his song.

"Darlin', no dad wants to see his little girl grow up, but every dad knows someday she has to," Mr. Stewart said. "When this plane lands in Denver, I'm getting off . . . and you're staying on and going to Florida."

Miley's mouth fell open. This was not what she had been expecting to hear. "Are you sure?" she asked her dad in disbelief.

"I've never been more sure of anything," Mr. Stewart said sincerely. "Besides, Hannah Montana don't need no Daddy to hang around to go down there and show that Mikayla what she's made of."

"Oh, Dad," said Miley, giving him a hug. He grunted in pain. "Sorry," she said.

"That's okay," responded Mr. Stewart. "It's a good kind of pain." They hugged again. Miley picked up the motion-sickness bag reverently. "I'm going to save this forever," she told her dad.

Just then Roxy stumbled by their seats, clutching her stomach. The freebies in first class had finally taken their toll. "Oh, no," she groaned. "Shrimp and cookies: bad combo." She grabbed the bag out of Miley's hand and ran to the bathroom.

Oh, no! Miley looked at her dad, stricken.

"It's okay," said Mr. Stewart. He patted his heart. "I got it all in here." He reached over, and he and Miley shared another hug.

But their tender moment quickly came to a close as Roxy's voice rang out from the bathroom. "I'm gonna need a bigger barf bag!" she cried.

Mr. Stewart and Jackson were back at home. Mr. Stewart was on the phone with Miley, once again upside down on the table. All those hours squeezed into coach left his back in worse pain than ever. His hair stood straight up. "Lilly and I just watched the concert on TV," he said. "You were terrific."

Lilly bent over backward to talk into the phone. "And you blew Mikayla off the stage!" she squealed.

Mr. Stewart frowned. That wasn't the point he was trying to make. "The important thing is, honey, you did a great thing for charity," he said. He then held the phone out for Lilly.

"And you blew Mikayla off the stage!" she squealed again.

"Yeah," Mr. Stewart agreed. "I guess Hannah did show her a thing or two. And my daughter did the same for me. I'm proud of you, darling."

Lilly leaned in again. "And . . ." she started to say. "You blew Mikayla off the stage!" she and Mr. Stewart said in unison.

"Hey, Jackson!" called Mr. Stewart. "Your sister is on the phone. You want to say hello?"

"Uh, can't right now!" Jackson called back. "Kinda busy!"

He stood on the deck next to the Solo-Bend-A-Flex 5000. Rico was sitting on the machine, and Jackson was giving him the hard sell. "So trust me, Rico," said Jackson. "A couple of workouts on this bad boy, and you are gonna be Mr. Irresistible."

Rico was skeptical. "I don't know," he said. "Doesn't feel like it's doing anything."

"Well let me just turn it up for you a little, kid," said Jackson, as he started to spin the adjustment wheel.

Oops! Jackson ducked as Rico went sailing off the machine.

"Waaaaaa!" Rico cried. He landed in the sand, then popped right back up.

"Whoa!" he cried. "That was awesome!" He ran back to the house. "Again Jackson! Again! Again!"

Put your hands together for the next Hannah Montana book . . .

Game of Hearts

Adapted by M. C. King

Based on the series created by Michael Poryes and Rich Correll & Barry O'Brien

Based on the episode, "You Are So Sue-able to Me," Written by Sally Lapiduss

Sometimes guys could be so immature. Miley Stewart had seen her share of grossness in the school cafeteria, but this was extreme. She sat in baffled silence, her fork poised above her plate, watching two guys at the next table lob meatballs into each other's mouths. "He goes from the top of the key, he shoots, he scores!" Nick shouted. Todd caught the meatball in his gaping mouth, then grinned proudly. Tomato sauce dribbled down his chin. *Ugh*, thought Miley, feeling nauseous. *Where were these guys raised? A barn?*

"I can't believe Justin Timberlake is from the same species. Some boys are such pigs," she said with a frown, then turned toward her best friend, Lilly Truscott.

But Lilly hadn't heard her. She was totally focused on her lunch. Spaghetti strands dangled from Lilly's lips as she slowly slurped. Miley couldn't believe her eyes. Or her ears! Lilly was slurping with gusto—and volume! What was happening? Was it Be-as-Disgusting-as-You-Can-Be day at school today? "Lilly!" Miley saying in a raised voice.

A distracted Lilly looked up from her plate. "Wha?" she grumbled, her mouth full of spaghetti.

"Close your mouth!" Miley exclaimed. She couldn't help feeling a little embarrassed for Lilly. "We're in the ninth grade. You gotta start acting more like a, oh, I don't know . . . a girl?"

Lilly scowled, tugging at the ski cap she was wearing over her tangled, unbrushed hair. "What are you talking about? I act like a girl all the time."

"Incoming!" they heard Todd scream, as a meatball flew toward them. Miley braced herself for the splat, while Lilly leaped to her feet and with expert precision caught the meatball one-handed. "Truscott from downtown!" she yelled, shooting it into Todd's mouth. "Boo-yah!" she hooted triumphantly. She ran over to give the guys high fives.

Lilly caught Miley staring at a spaghetti stain on her sweatshirt and her face turned bright red. "I know how to be a girl," she exclaimed defensively.

Sometimes you had to be brutally honest with your best friend—no matter how painful the consequences. "Then how come you don't have a date for the dance Friday night?" Miley asked Lilly.

"Not everybody's going to the dance," Lilly huffed. "*You're* not going."

Miley lowered her voice. "I've got a Hannah Montana concert," she whispered.

Miley saw the crestfallen look on Lilly's face. "I'm not going to let you give up," she said encouragingly. "There's a ninth grade girl in there and I'm going to get her out."